Bertie the Basset

By

Andrea Barclay

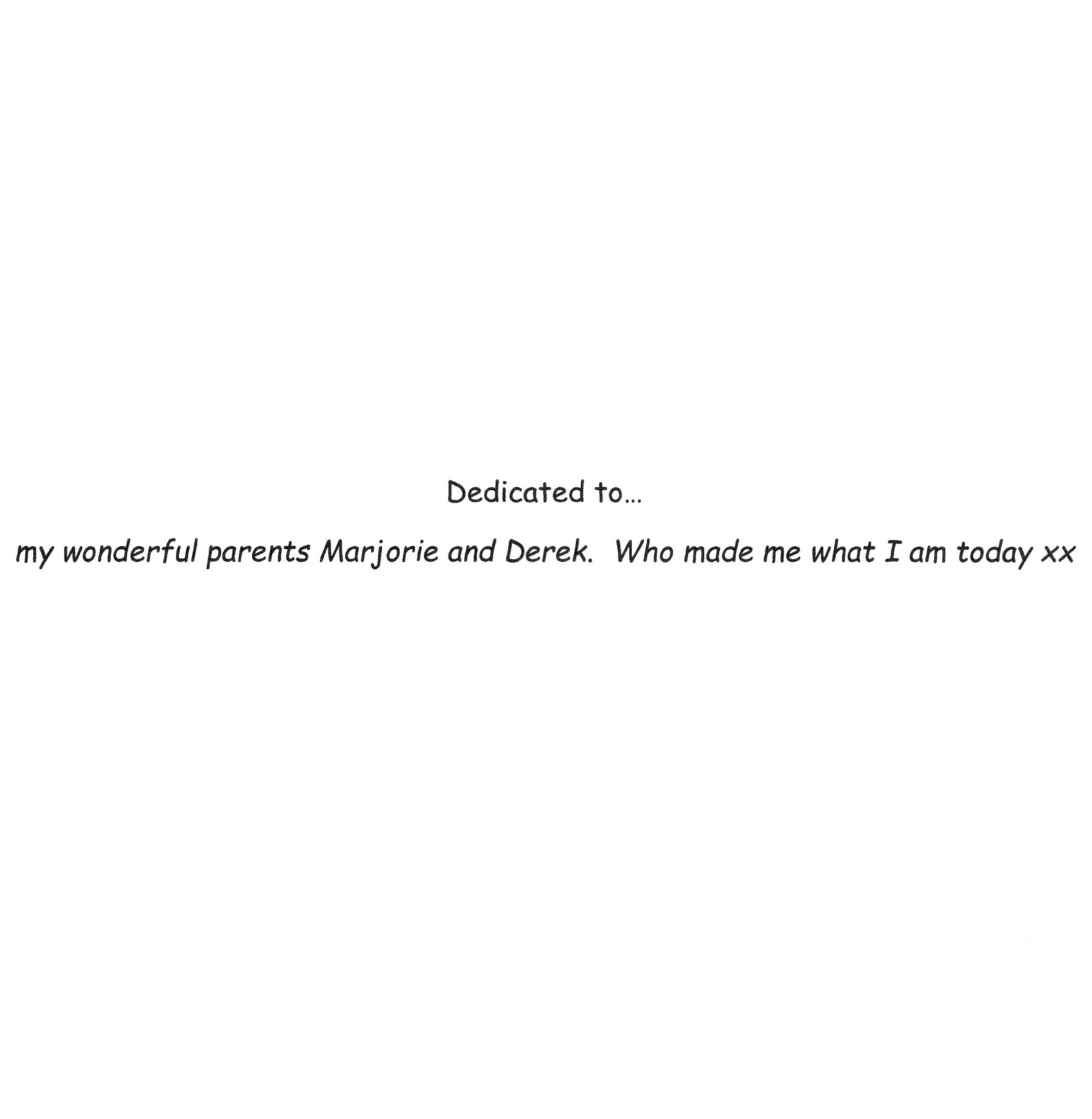

Dedicated to…

my wonderful parents Marjorie and Derek. Who made me what I am today xx

Bertie the Basset

Bertie the Basset wanted some fun,

As he wriggled around in the midday sun,

Bertie was thinking of something nice,

But Tiggy the cat said, "let's chase mice",

Bertie thought and then said "I know,

We can hop on a bus and go and see a show?"

Tiggy the cat said, "How can we do that?",

"Don't forget that I am just a cat!",

Tiggy just lay there and thought for a while,

But Bertie the Basset just looked up and smiled,

Bertie the Basset he had a plan,

For he knew of a man named Stan.

And Stan had a car that was bright blue,

And Stan shouted out "Come on you two",

The car had no roof and Bertie's ears they did flap,

But Tiggy the cat just wanted to nap,

So off they raced Stan and Bertie,

They drove very fast and got very dirty.

The wind and the dust were all in Stans Hair,

But Bertie the Basset he did not care,

He was out in the car and having some fun,

 Just like he wanted in the midday sun.

But Stan had forgotten one thing that day,

He was driving so fast he had lost his way.

Bertie the Basset was trying to be brave,

When all of a sudden, they saw Dave,

Dave the Donkey was plodding along,

With a face so sad and so long,

Bertie the Basset called out "Dave it's me",

Dave the donkey looked up to see.

Bertie the Basset asked Dave the way home,

"I'm getting hungry and don't have my phone",

"I will help you home, if you will help me",

"I have a problem today you see",

"I've lost my tail and am so sad",

"It was the best tail I ever had!".

But Bertie the Basset knew something Dave had forgotten,

Dave's pink tail was attached to his bottom,

Dave was so happy he jumped up and down,

"Now I no longer have to frown".

"I am so happy and now not sad",

Dave said, "Bertie you are a great friend to have",

Dave the donkey said, "I will take you back home",

"And then you can have your tasty bone".

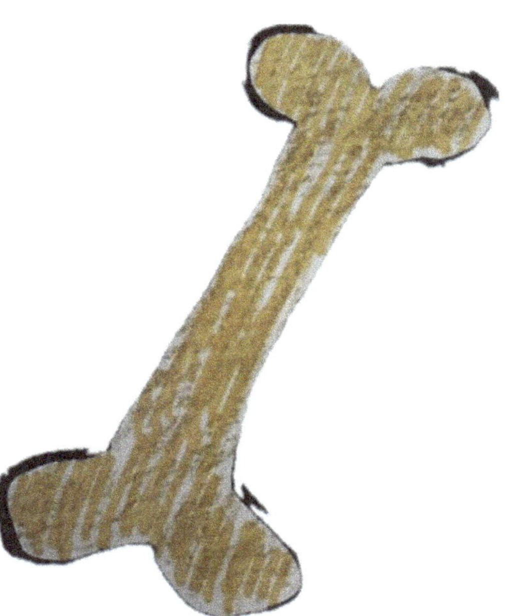

Bertie in the park

Bertie the Basset went

for a walk, with his best friend

 Michael the Mouse,

They wanted to play

football in the park

that day,So, they called at

another friend's house,

And who do you think lived in that house?

No other than George the Giraffe,

They knocked on the door,

but no answer came, as

 George he was in the bath,

"George", shouted Bertie

"When you are free, do you

want to play football with us?".

But before he could answer

along came Paul hopping off the bus,

Paul was a peacock with a bright blue tail,

and he loved football as well,

So now there were four they still

needed four more then they

suddenly heard a bell.

A bicycle whizzed by and sat

on the seat was another friend

Humphrey the Hippo,

Humphrey wanted to play too

so he asked"Can I bring my
brother Biffo?"

Biffo and Humphrey were twin
hippos

and they both liked to play in goal.

Then Bertie the basset so

pleased with himself nearly fell down a hole,

"We still need two more, does

anyone know of any other

friends who can play?"

"I do" said Paul "And he's in the park

my really good friend Ray".

Ray was a rabbit with a fluffy

white tail, and he loved to play up front,

So all afternoon they played together

and had such a lot of fun,

And when it was time to go in for tea

Bertie the Basset was sad

But not for long because it was

the best day that he ever had.

Bertie and the Balloon

Bertie the Basset was on the phone,

to his good friend Freddie the Frog,

They decided to meet but instead

of a walk, Freddie he wanted to jog,

He jogged along and saw a bee on

a beautiful yellow sunflower.

But as he looked the bumblebee shook

and gave Freddie the frog a shower,

Freddie was cross and started to

shout but the bumblebee she just smiled

"Why are you cross, Freddie the frog?

I am only meek and mild"

"I wanted a jog and not a

 swim" Freddie the frog replied,

But his frown soon turned

upside down as the little

bumble   bee cried,

"I'm not cross little bumblebee,

in fact you made me smile"

"I was getting hot with all

this jogging, and I've

already finished my mile",

Now in the distance they

 saw Bertie the Basset and

he was holding a balloon,

He was about to give this to

Freddie the frog

 when it was taken by a baboon.

"Bobby the baboon, that's

not your balloon, I bought

it for Freddie the frog",

But Bobby just ran as fast

as he could much faster than a
jog,

Then all of a sudden, they

heard a bang and

Bobby started to cry.

So never take a frog's balloon

unless you have a good reason why,

Now Bobby came back all

ashamed his face as red

as his bottom,

And this was never spoken

about again in fact it's completely forgotten.